A Story a Day 'Til Christmas

Edited by Nan Roloff

Current

ILLUSTRATORS

The Candles—Linda Griffith
Christmas Every Day—Christina Ljungren Rigo
St. Nicholas' Eve in Hans Brinker's Day—Cheryl Harness
A Gift for Mr. Guerney—Peggy Toole
An Alphabet of Christmas—Peggy Toole
The Fuzzy Little Christmas—Deborah Colvin Borgo
Long, Long Ago—Kristin Kennedy
The Tree That Didn't Get Trimmed—Tim O'Toole
Why the Chimes Rang—Peggy Toole
Christmas Among the Animals—Don Eberhart
Christmas Underground—Linda Kenagy
Yes, Virginia, There is a Santa Claus—John Baumbach
A Very Murray Christmas—Pam Fouts
Grandma's Fast-Food Christmas Dinner—Bill Stroble
The Gift of the Magi—Mark Dixon
Christmas Bells—Don Eberhart
How Saint Francis Told the Christmas Story—Bill Stroble
Santa Gets the Bug—Phil Fickling
The Holy Night—Linda Griffith
The Christmas Story—Drew Smith
At Christmas, Anything Can Happen—Pam Peltier
Christmas is for Children—Jan Gregg
The Christmas Cuckoo—Peggy Toole
The Night Before Christmas—Marsha Howe
Cover and title page—Peggy Toole

Book Design—Jean James

TABLE OF CONTENTS

The Candles

There was once a big wax candle that was quite proud of itself. "I am made of wax and have been cast, not dipped," it said. "My light is clearer and I burn longer than other candles. I belong in a chandelier or a silver candlestick."

"That must be lovely," said the humble tallow candle. "I am only made of tallow, but I have been dipped eight times instead of two like most. So I have a decent waistline and am satisfied. Wax candles are put in the living room and I have to stay in the kitchen, but that is a good place, too. It is warm and friendly and is where all the food is prepared."

"There are certainly more important things in life than food," sniffed the wax candle, "things like parties and dancing. There is going to be a Christmas ball tonight. At any moment they will come for me and my whole family."

Hardly had this been said when the lady of the house came to get the wax candles, but she took the little tallow candle, too. She brought it into the kitchen where a little boy stood with a basket on his arm. It was filled with potatoes and a few apples. All this the kind mistress had given the poor boy. "Here, my little friend," she said, and she put the tallow candle into his basket. "I know your mother often works so late into the night." Her little daughter, who was standing nearby, smiled when she heard her mother say "so late into the night."

"We are going to have a party! And my dress has red bows on it, and I will be allowed to be up so late into the night," she said joyfully. Her eyes sparkled with expectation, she was so happy. Not even wax candles can shine like the eyes of a child.

"That was a blessed sight," thought the tallow candle. "I shall never forget it, nor am I likely to see such happiness again."

The boy went on his way and the tallow candle went with him.

"I wonder where I'm going," it thought. "Probably to people so poor they don't even have a brass candlestick; while the wax candle sits in silver and is in the finest company. Well, it is my lot in life to be tallow and not wax."

And the tallow candle was brought to a poor home where a widow lived with her three children. From their rooms, with their low ceilings and narrow windows, they could look across the street to the great house.

"God bless her who gave you this," said the

boy's mother when she saw the tallow candle. "It will burn late into the night." And the candle was lit.

In the rich house the wax candles were also lit. From the windows their light fell out into the street. Coaches rumbled along the cobblestones as they arrived, bringing elegantly dressed guests, and soon music was heard.

"Now the ball is starting," thought the tallow candle, recalling the little rich girl with the sparkling eyes. "I shall never see eyes like those again."

The youngest of the poor woman's children was a girl, too. She put her arms around her brother and sister and whispered to them, "We are going to have hot potatoes for dinner." Her eyes looked bright and happy, too, just as happy as the little girl's across the street had looked when she spoke of her bows.

The table was set. The potatoes were eaten. How good they tasted! And then there were apples for dessert. The youngest child recited a little verse:

> *Dear God, thanks to Your will,*
> *I once more my stomach did fill.*
> *Amen*

"Did I say it nicely?" the girl asked her mother.

The mother smiled and shook her head. "That you mustn't ask or think about. What is important is to be thankful to God for what He does for us."

The children were tucked into bed and each given a kiss, then they fell right to sleep. The mother stayed up and sewed late into the night. She had to earn a living for herself and her children. Over in the house of the rich the wax candles were still burning and the music played. Above in the sky the stars shone, and they shone as brightly on the poor home as the rich one.

"That was a nice evening," thought the tallow candle. "I wonder if the wax candle had a better time in the silver candlestick? That is the question I would like to have answered before I am burned out." Then it thought of the two equally happy faces; one shining in the light of the wax candles and the other in the light of the tallow one, and its flame danced brightly, and even a bit proudly, before its light disappeared forever into the darkness of that Christmas night.

by Hans Christian Andersen

Christmas Every Day

Once there was a little girl who liked Christmas so much she wanted it to be Christmas every day. And as soon as Thanksgiving was over she began to send letters to Santa to ask if it could be so. Just the day before Christmas, she got a letter from Santa saying she could have Christmas every day for one whole year—then they would see about having it longer.

The little girl was already very excited, getting ready for the old-fashioned, once-a-year Christmas that was coming the next day, so

perhaps Santa's promise didn't impress her like it should have. She simply decided to keep the secret to herself and surprise everyone as it kept coming true. Then she forgot all about it!

She had a wonderful Christmas. She went to bed early so Santa could have a chance to fill the stockings, and in the morning she was up first to peek into them and find a coin purse and a rubber ball and candy and all kinds of small presents. Then she waited till the rest of the family woke up, and she burst into the library to look at the large presents—dolls and a little stove and skates and a box of water-colors under the big sparkling tree.

She had a splendid Christmas all day. She ate so much candy that she didn't want any breakfast, and for dinner she ate turkey and cranberries and plum pudding and nuts and raisins and more candy. Then she went out sledding and came in crying with a stomach-ache; and her daddy said was it any wonder and they all went to bed cross.

The little girl slept very heavily and very late the next morning—but she was awakened at last by the other children dancing around her bed with their stockings full of presents in their hands.

"What is it?" cried the little girl as she rub-bed her eyes.

"Christmas! Christmas! Christmas!" they all shouted and waved their stockings.

All at once it occurred to the little girl that Santa had kept his promise, and her year of Christmases was beginning. She was dreadfully tired, but she sprang up and darted to the library. There it was again! Books and dolls and paints—

There was the Christmas tree blazing away, and the family picking out their presents, but looking pretty sleepy, and her father confused and her mother ready to cry. "What am I going to do with all these things?!" said her mother, and her father said it seemed to him like they had just had something like this the day before, but he must have dreamed it.

The next day it was the same thing over again, but everyone was getting cross; and at the end of the week, so many people lost their tempers that the little girl became frightened, keeping the secret all to herself. She wanted to tell her mother, but she didn't dare, and she was ashamed to ask Santa to take back the gift. So it went on and on, and it was Christmas on Valentine's Day and Washington's Birthday and even April Fool's Day.

Turkeys got to be a thousand dollars apiece and cranberries went for a diamond apiece. All the woods and orchards were cut down for Christmas trees, leaving nothing but fields of stumps, and after a while they had to make Christmas trees out of rags and stuff them with bran. But there were plenty of rags because people got so poor, buying presents for one another, they couldn't afford new clothes and just wore their old ones to tatters.

After four months, the little girl, whenever she saw those ugly great lumpy stockings dan-gling at the fireplace and saw those disgusting presents around everywhere, burst into tears. In six months she was perfectly exhausted and just lay around rolling her eyes and panting. By October she took to sitting down on her dolls, she hated the sight of them so, and by Thanksgiving she was disgusted and just slam-med her presents across the room.

By that time people didn't deliver presents nicely anymore, but flung them over the fence or through the window saying, "Take it, you horrid thing!"

Well, around Thanksgiving it had leaked out who had caused all the Christmases. Hardly anyone would play with the little girl. People perfectly despised her, for if it hadn't been for her greediness, all these Christmases never would have happened. The little girl began sending letters to Santa, and then telegrams, begging him to stop. But all she got back were messages like "not at home" or "otherwise engaged."

Finally, one night the little girl fell asleep, and when she woke up, it wasn't Christmas anymore. There was rejoicing everywhere. People hugged each other and cried and kissed for joy. The city carts went around and gath-ered up all the candy and raisins and nuts and dumped them into the river, making the fish perfectly sick.

The little girl went to thank Santa for stopping Christmas and asked him to make sure Christmas never, ever came again. But he frowned and asked if she was sure that was what she wanted. "Why not?" the little girl asked. And Santa said now she was behaving as selfishly as before, so she said how about once a year like it used to be. Santa said that was the good old way that had pleased people ever since Christmas began and agreed. Then the little girl gave Santa a great big hug and skipped the whole way home, she was so glad.

St. Nicholas' Eve in Hans Brinker's Day

It has been said that our Santa Claus originally came from Holland. In America Santa comes rollicking along on the 25th of December, our holy Christmas morn; but in Holland, St. Nicholas visits earth on the 5th, a time set aside especially for him. Early on the morning of the 6th, which is St. Nicholas Day, he distributes his candies, toys, and treasures, then vanishes for a year.

Christmas Day in Holland is devoted to church rites and family visiting. It is on St. Nicholas' Eve that their young people become half wild with joy and expectation. To some it is a sorry time, for the saint is very honest, and, if anyone has been naughty during the past year, he is sure to tell them so. Sometimes he even carries a birch rod under his arm, and advises parents to give scoldings in place of candies and whippings instead of toys!

The van Gleck children were very excited on this St. Nicholas' Eve. They had been admitted into the grand parlor: they were dressed in their best and had been given two cakes apiece at supper. Father, Mother and Grandmother looked over their merry games with approval while Grandfather napped with his large red handkerchief over his face.

Now the spirit of fun reigned supreme. The very flames danced in the polished fireplace grate as a pair of prim candles winked at each other. At last the children grew so uproarious

that the grandsire's red kerchief came down from his face with a jerk. Who could sleep in such a racket! It was high time to attend to business. Mother suggested that, if they wished to see the good St. Nicholas, they should sing the same loving invitation that had brought him the year before.

The children, each holding a pretty willow basket, formed at once in a ring. Mother began playing softly upon the piano: soon the gentle, childish voices rose—

Welcome, friend! St. Nicholas, welcome!
Bring no rod for us tonight!
While our voices bid thee welcome,
Every heart with joy is light.

Tell us every fault and failing;
We will bear thy keenest railing.
So we sing, so we sing:
Thou shalt tell us everything!

Welcome, friend! St. Nicholas, welcome!
Welcome to this merry band!
Happy children greet thee, welcome!
Thou art gladdening all the land.

Fill each empty hand and basket;
'Tis thy little ones who ask it.
So we sing, so we sing:
Thou wilt bring us everything!

During the chorus, various glances, half in eagerness, half in dread, were cast towards the polished folding-doors. Now a loud knocking was heard. The circle was broken in an instant. Little ones pressed against their mother's knee while the others settled themselves around Father expectantly.

The knocking was heard again.

"Come in," said Mother softly.

The door slowly opened; and St. Nicholas, in full array, stood before them. You could have heard a pin drop. Soon he spoke. What a mysterious majesty in his voice! What kindliness in his tones!

"Karel van Gleck, I am pleased to greet thee and thy honored wife. Children, I greet ye all—Hendrick, Hilda, Broom, Katy, Huygens, and Lucretia. And thy cousins—Wolfert, Diedrich, Mayken, Voost and Katrina. Good children ye have been, in the main, since I last saw ye. Diedrich was rude at the Haarlem fair last fall; but he has tried to atone for it since. Mayken has failed, of late, in her lessons; and too many sweets and trifles have gone to her lips. Diedrich, I trust, will be a polite, manly boy for the future; and Mayken will try to shine as a student. Little Katy has been cruel to the cat more than once. St. Nicholas can hear the cat cry when its tail is pulled. I will forgive her, if she will remember from this hour that the smallest dumb creatures have feelings, and must not be abused."

As Katy burst into a frightened cry, the saint graciously remained silent until she was soothed.

"Master Broom," he resumed, "I warn thee that boys who are in the habit of putting snuff upon the foot-stove of the school-mistress may one day be discovered and receive a spanking." (Master Broom colored, and stared in great astonishment.) "But thou art such an excellent scholar, I shall make thee no further reproof."

"Thou, Hendrick, didst distinguish thyself in the archery match last spring, and hit a bulls-eye. I give thee credit for excelling in manly sport and exercise; though I must not unduly approve thy boat-racing, since it leaves thee too little time for studies.

"Lucretia and Hilda shall have a blessed sleep tonight. Their kindness to the poor, and

cheerful, hearty obedience, will render them happy.

"With one and all I avow myself well content. Goodness, industry, benevolence, and thrift have prevailed in your midst. Therefore, my blessings upon you; and may the New Year find all treading the paths of obedience, wisdom, and love! Tomorrow you shall find more substantial proof that I have been in your midst. Farewell!"

With these words came a great shower of sugarplums upon the linen sheet spread out in front of the doors. A general scramble followed as the children fairly tumbled over each other in their eagerness to fill their baskets. Then the bravest of the youngsters sprang up and burst open the closed doors. In vain they searched for St. Nicholas, but he was nowhere to be seen.

Soon there was a rush into another room, where stood a table covered with the finest, white linen damask. Excitedly each child laid a shoe upon it. The door was then carefully locked, and its key hidden in Mother's bedroom. Next followed goodnight kisses, a grand family procession to the upper floor, merry farewells at bedroom doors, and then silence, at last, fell over the van Gleck mansion.

Early the next morning the door was solemnly unlocked and opened in the presence of the assembled household; when, lo! a sight appeared, proving St. Nicholas to be a saint of his word.

Every shoe was filled to overflowing; and beside each stood many a colored pile. The table was heavy with its load of presents—candies, toys, trinkets, books, and other articles. Everyone had gifts, from Grandfather to the baby . . . "Oh!" and "Ah!" the children cried over their treasures . . . and frolic and joy reigned supreme.

Good St. Nicholas! For the sake of young Hollanders, I, for one, am willing to acknowledge him, and defend his reality against all unbelievers.

Cheryl Harness

A Gift for Mr. Guerney

There was once a young girl named Charlotte who especially liked an old man named Mr. Guerney who lived about a mile away from her. So Charlotte made four gingerbread men to take to him for Christmas.

Charlotte carefully wrapped the gingerbread men in red and green tissue, put on her warm coat and scarf and mittens, and left on a blustery day for Mr. Guerney's house. She walked a little ways until she saw a dog sitting in the snow. "Owwoooo," howled the dog, and he looked so cold that Charlotte felt sorry for him, so she gave him a gingerbread man to eat.

Now Charlotte had three gingerbread men for Mr. Guerney. But soon she heard a loud chattering and twirping. Walking up to a snow-filled bush she saw Mrs. Bloom's big old Tomcat circling around on the ground, eyeing a chickadee in the branches. "Oh, go on!" Charlotte chased the Tom away. She wondered why the chickadee couldn't fly and thought maybe he needed some food. So Charlotte crumbled up a gingerbread man and left it beneath the bush for the bird.

Now Charlotte had two gingerbread men for Mr. Guerney. She had almost reached his house when she heard some sniffles and whimpers. Then she saw little, four-year-old Lorry Simpson crying in her front yard. Lorry's big brother, David, had gone sledding and told her she was too little to go. "Oh, dear," said Charlotte, and she gave Lorry a gingerbread man, the cutest one with the red eyes and the raisin nose.

Now Charlotte had only one gingerbread man left, and she had meant to bring four! Oh no, she thought, one gingerbread man wasn't much of a gift for such a good friend as Mr. Guerney.

Mr. Guerney smiled broadly when he saw Charlotte. "Come in, come in," he said. His eyes twinkled as she told him she only had one gingerbread man for him, but she had started out with four. He fixed them some hot chocolate to enjoy as they shared the last gingerbread man, and Charlotte told Mr. Guerney about the dog and the chickadee and little Lorry Simpson. They had a very nice visit, and when Charlotte left Mr. Guerney said, "Charlotte, you gave me one gingerbread man and three stories. That's better than four gingerbread men. In fact, that's the best present I've had all year."

Charlotte smiled happily. Maybe, she thought, next year I'll make five gingerbread men.

An Alphabet of Christmas

A   is for Animals who shared the stable.
B   for the Babe with their manger for cradle.
C   for the Carols so blithe and gay.
D   for December, the twenty-fifth day.
E   for the Eve when we're all so excited.
F   for the Fun when the tree's at last lighted.
G   is for Goose which you all know is fat.
H   is the Holly you stick in your hat.
I   for the Ivy that clings to the wall.
J   is for Jesus, the cause of it all.
K   for the Kindness begot by this feast.
L   is for Light shining way in the East.
M   for the Mistletoe, all green and white.
N   for the Noels we sing Christmas night.
O   for the Oxen, the first to adore Him.
P   for the Presents Wise Men laid before Him.
Q   for the Quiet of this holy Eve
        as God's greatest blessing we all did receive.
R   for the Reindeer leaping over the roofs.
S   for the Stockings that Santa Claus stuffs.
T   for the Toys, the Tinsel, the Tree.
U   is for Us—the whole family.
V   is for Visitors bringing us cheer.
W   is Welcome to the happy New Year.
X   **YZ** bother me! So now
        to you all, wherever you be,
        a merry, merry Christmas,
        and many may you see!

The Fuzzy Little Christmas

Rupert G. (as in Grumpy) Bear slumped in the corner of the toy shelf and grumbled to himself.

"Humphh—here it is, Christmas again. Sarah is having a great time baking cookies, wrapping presents . . . All *I* get to do is sit here in this dusty old corner. Christmas is lots more fun for kids than it is for fuzzy ol' bears." With that, he crossed his paws over his tubby bear tummy and went "hmphh-hmpph-hmpph!"

"Oh, what is it *now*, Rupert!?" sniffed Maybelle, the porcelain doll, from her specially made pedestal.

"It's not fair for Sarah to have all the fun while we're stuck up here! We'll be lucky if she even remembers to take us to look at the tree—and just wait till all the new toys get here!"

Rupert was getting more worked up by the minute.

"Tut-tut! You're so insecure, Rupert. I'm certainly not worried about anyone replacing me." Maybelle returned her lips to their perfect pout.

"Thanks for being so understanding, Maybelle! Sorry I mentioned it! Just forget it, okay?!" Rupert grumped. "I wish Christmas was over!"

Downstairs in the living room, Sarah was helping her parents decorate the tree while her spotted pup, Clarence, poked his nose into the boxes of ornaments scattered on the floor. How fragrant the soft green needles smelled as each branch was carefully draped with silvery tinsel streamers. Old-fashioned lights bubbled merrily on the boughs, reflecting shimmering

colors on the delicate glass balls.

"It's so beautiful!" gasped Sarah. "I must go get Rupert so he can see it, too!"

Rupert heard Sarah's little footsteps running up the stairs. "Here we go again," he muttered as he felt her little hands tugging him down from his spot. "Ye-ouch!" winced Rupert as he thump-bumped his way to the floor.

In the living room Sarah held up Rupert so he could admire the beautiful tree.

"I suppose I should feel honored," Rupert sulked.

"Oh, Rupert! Isn't it the most wonderful tree you ever saw?" sighed little Sarah, hugging him tightly.

"Yeah—and I bet it was fun to decorate," Rupert wanted to say, "but then, *I* wouldn't know about that!"

"Time to put the angel on top, Sweetie," said Sarah's daddy. Her mommy looked around and said, "The box was right here a minute ago . . ."

From under the tree, they could see Clarence's little puppy tail swishing back and forth, back and forth. He was busy at work on something. Playfully he poked his head out from under the tree and grinned, his mouth covered with bits of yarn and glitter. Angela, the Christmas angel, lay battered and dazed beneath the tree, in a state of shock from an onslaught of doggy kisses.

"Clarence! What have you done!" cried Daddy, Mommy and Sarah all together. With his tail between his legs, a shamefaced Clarence was banished to the garage.

Everyone slumped down onto the couch while Angela stared up at them with rumpled hair and a crumpled halo. Even Rupert felt sorry for her. "She's going to need a l-o-n-g vacation to get over this," he thought.

"Well, I think I can repair her hair," sighed Mommy, "but it will take a while. At least nothing else is damaged. But I don't know what we're going to do for now . . ."

Sarah brushed her cheek against Rupert's fuzzy little bear head, then sat back and plopped Angela's halo over one of his ears. "I think my Rupert would make a wonderful Christmas angel."

"Who, ME?!!" gasped Rupert to himself. "Good grief!" He was about to roll his eyes when he found himself staring nose-to-nose at Mommy. Carefully she removed the velvet angel dress from Angela and slipped it onto Rupert's fuzzy bear body. Rupert hoped she didn't notice that he was holding in his tubby bear tummy as best he could. Next, Mommy pinned the delicate angel wings to the back of the dress without sticking Rupert, much to his relief. As she set the halo straight, she said, "You know, I usually don't think of Rupert as the angelic type, but I think he might do."

"What's *that* supposed to mean!" huffed Rupert.

Daddy lifted Rupert to the very tip of the tree where he was gently tied on with shiny gold cord. As everyone stepped back to judge the results, Rupert stuck out his fuzzy little bear chest and tried to look as sweet as possible. "Perfect!" declared Daddy.

So there was Rupert, gracing the top of the soft, fragrant and somewhat tickly tree as the lights and tinsel danced beneath him.

"Wow! If only Maybelle could see me on MY pedestal," thought Rupert. "Why, I not only got to decorate the tree, I'm a decoration!" His fuzzy little bear heart swelled with pride as he surveyed the glorious sight of which he was a part. "Look at me, Rupert G. (as in Grumpy) Bear . . ." he smiled. "Hm-m-m . . . maybe I ought to change the G. to stand for Grand!"

Long, Long Ago

Winds through the olive trees
   Softly did blow,
Round little Bethlehem
   Long, long ago.

Sheep on the hillside lay
   Whiter than snow;
Shepherds were watching them
   Long, long ago.

Then from the happy sky,
   Angels bent low,
Singing their songs of joy
   Long, long ago.

For in a manger bed,
   Cradled we know,
Christ came to Bethlehem
   Long, long ago.

The Tree That Didn't Get Trimmed

All young fir trees dream of being Christmas trees. With that vision of merriment before them, they endure the sharp sting of the ax and the long hours pressed together on a freight car. But every Christmas, there are more trees cut down than are needed. And that is the story no one has ever thought to put down.

The tree in this story should never have been cut. He wouldn't have been, but it was getting dark in the Vermont woods and the man with the ax said, "Just one more."

He was a fine, well-grown youngster, but too tall for his age; his branches were rather scraggly. If he'd been left there he would have been an unusually big tree some day; but now he was in the awkward age and didn't have a tapering shape and the thick, even foliage that people like on trees. Worse still, instead of running up to a straight, clean spire, his tip was a bit lop-sided, with a fork in it.

But he didn't know this as he stood with many others, leaning against the side wall of the grocer's shop. In those cold December days he was very happy, thinking of the pleasures to come. He had heard of the delights of Christmas Eve: the setting up of the tree, the tinsel balls and colored toys and stars and peppermint canes and birds with spun-glass tails.

"I shall be very grand," he said. "I hope there will be children to admire me." He even felt sorry for the first trees that were chosen and taken away. It would be best, he felt, not to be bought until Christmas Eve. Then, in the shining darkness someone would pick him out, put him carefully along the running board of a car and away they would go.

The tire-chains would clack and jingle merrily on the snowy road. He imagined a big house with a fire glowing in the hearth, the hushed rustle of wrapping paper and parcels being unpacked. Someone would say, "Oh, what a beautiful tree!" How erect and stiff he would brace himself in his iron tripod stand.

But day after day went by, one by one the other trees were taken, and he began to grow troubled. For everyone who looked at him had an unkind word. "Too tall," or "too skimpy," or "that top will never do." The grocer pushed him back carelessly and he toppled over and fell alongside the wall. No one bothered to pick him up. He was almost glad, for now his pride would be spared.

Now it was Christmas Eve. It was a foggy evening with a drizzling rain; the alley alongside the store was thick with trampled slush. As he lay there among the broken boxes and fallen scraps of holly, strange thoughts came to him. In the still, northern forest already his wounded stump was buried in forgetful snow. He remembered the wintry sparkle of the woods, the big trees with crusts and clumps of silver on their broad boughs, the keen singing of the lonely wind. He remembered the strong, warm feeling of his roots reaching down into the safe earth. And he had given it all up to be here, disdained and forgotten, in a littered alley. The splash of feet, the boom of bells, the cry of cars went past him. He trembled with self-pity and vexation. "No toys and stockings for me," he thought sadly, and shed some of his needles.

Late that night, the grocer came out to clear away what was left. The boxes, broken wreaths, empty barrels and our tree with one or two others were all thrown through the side door into the cellar. The door was locked and he lay there in the dark. "So this is Christmas," he said to himself.

All Christmas Day it was very still in the cellar. Feet went along the pavement above, and there was the chiming of church bells. The unwanted trees lay on the stone floor, watching the furnace flicker.

The day after Christmas a man came in who wanted some greenery to decorate a cemetery. The grocer seized an ax and—chop, chop, chop—the sweet-smelling branches of the leftover trees were carried away. The naked trunks were thrown in the corner, but the trees were too disheartened to care.

Now our tree had plenty of time to think. How silly he had been to imagine such a fine career for himself. He felt sorry for the other young trees, still growing in the fresh, hilly country, who were enjoying the same fantastic dream.

Then one day a farmer came to the grocer's and the naked, dusty fir-poles were thrown into a truck with many others and made a rattling journey into the country. The farmer unloaded them in his yard and was stacking them when his wife came out. "There!" she said. "That's just what I need, a nice long pole with a fork in it. Jim, put that one over there to hold up the clothesline." It was the first time anyone had praised the tree, and his dried-up heart swelled with the tingle of forgotten sap. They put him near one end of the clothesline, with his stump close to a flower bed. It was wash-day, and soon the farmer's wife began bringing out wet garments to swing and freshen in the clean, bright air. The very first thing she hung near the top of the Christmas pole was a cluster of children's stockings.

Our tree was so cheerful watching the stockings and other bright little clothes plumped out in the wind that he didn't notice what was going on below him. A vine had caught hold of his trunk and was steadily twisting upward. And one morning, when the farmer's wife came out intending to shift him, she stopped and exclaimed. "Why, I mustn't move this pole—the morning glory has run right up it." So it had, and our bare pole was blue and green with color.

Something nice, the old firs believe, always happens to the trees that don't get trimmed. They even believe that some day one of the Christmas tree poles will be the starting point for another Magic Beanstalk, as in the fairy tale of the boy who climbed up the beanstalk and killed the giant. When that happens, fairy tales will begin all over again.

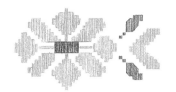

Why the Chimes Rang

There was once, in a far-away country where few people have ever traveled, a wonderful church. It stood on a high hill in the midst of a great city; and every Sunday, as well as on sacred days like Christmas, thousands of people climbed the hill to its great archways.

The building itself had stone columns and dark passages, and a main room so long, one could scarcely see from one end to the other. In the farthest corner was an organ so clear and loud, it could be heard for miles around. Altogether, no such church as this was ever seen before, especially when it was lighted up for some festival and crowded with people. But the strangest thing about the whole building was the wonderful bells.

At one corner of the church was a great gray tower that rose so far into the sky it was only in very fair weather that anyone could see the top. All the people knew that at the top of the tower were the Christmas bells. They had hung there since the church had been built, and had the most beautiful sound in the world. Some thought it was because a great musician had cast them and arranged them; others said it was because of the great height, which reached up where the air was clearest and purest: however that might be, everyone who had ever heard them thought they sounded like angels far up in the sky.

But the fact was that no one had heard them for years and years. They were Christmas chimes, you see, and were not meant to be played by men or on common days. It was the custom on Christmas Eve for all the people to bring to the church their offerings to the Christ-child; and when the greatest and best offering was laid on the altar, there used to come pealing through the music of the choir the Christmas chimes far up in the tower. Some said the wind rang them, and others said that

they were so high the angels set them swinging. But for many years they had never been heard. It was said that people had been growing less careful of their gifts for the Christ-child, and that no offering was brought that was great enough to deserve the music of the chimes.

Every Christmas the rich people still crowded the altar, each one trying to give a better gift than any other, without giving anything that he wanted for himself, and the church was crowded with those who thought perhaps the wonderful bells might be heard again. But although the service was splendid, and the offerings plenty, only the roar of the wind could be heard far up in the stone tower.

Now, a number of miles from the city, in a little country village where only glimpses of the tower could be seen in fair weather, there lived a boy named Pedro and his little brother. They knew very little about the Christmas chimes, but had heard of the Christmas service. Between them they formed a secret plan to go see the beautiful celebration.

"Nobody can guess, Little Brother," Pedro would say, "all the fine things there are to see and hear; and I have even heard it said that the Christ-child sometimes comes down to bless the service. What if we could see Him?"

The day before Christmas was bitterly cold, with a few lonely snowflakes flying in the air, and a hard white crust on the ground. Pedro and Little Brother were able to slip quietly away early in the afternoon; and although walking was hard in the frosty air, before nightfall they had trudged so far, hand in hand, that they saw the lights of the big city just ahead of them. Indeed, they were about to enter one of the great gates leading to the city when they saw a dark shape in the snow near their path, and stepped aside to look at it.

It was a poor woman who had fallen just outside the city too sick and tired to even seek shelter. She would soon be so sound asleep in the wintry air that no one would ever be able to awaken her again. All this Pedro saw in a moment, and he knelt down beside her and tried to rouse her. Turning her face toward him, he rubbed some snow on it, and when he had looked at her silently a moment he stood up again, and said: "It's no use, Little Brother. You will have to go alone."

"Alone?" cried Little Brother. "And you not see the Christmas festival?"

"No," said Pedro, with a bit of a choking sound in his throat. "See this poor woman. Her face looks like the Madonna in the chapel window, and she will freeze to death if nobody cares for her. Everyone has gone to the church now, but when you come back you can bring someone to help her. I will rub her to keep her from freezing, and perhaps get her to eat the bun that is left in my pocket."

"But I can not bear to leave you and go alone," said Little Brother.

"We both need not miss the service," said Pedro, "so you go. You can easily find your way to the church; and you must see everything twice, Little Brother—once for you and once for me. I am sure the Christ-child will know how I would love to come with you and worship Him; and oh! if you get a chance, Little Brother, to slip up to the altar without getting in anyone's way, take this little silver piece of mine and lay it down for my offering when no one is looking. Do not forget where you have left me, and forgive me for not going with you."

In this way he hurried Little Brother off to the city, and blinked hard to keep back the tears as he heard the crunching footsteps sounding farther and farther away in the twilight.

The great church was wonderful that night.

Everyone said it had never looked so beautiful. When the organ played and the thousands of people sang, the walls shook with sound, and little Pedro, away outside the city wall, felt the earth tremble around him.

At the close of the service came a procession with offerings to be laid on the altar. Rich men and great men proudly presented gifts of jewels and gold. Last of all walked the king of the country, hoping with all the rest to win for himself the chime of the Christmas bells. There went a great murmur through the crowd as the king took from his head the royal crown, all set with precious stones, and placed it gleaming on the altar. "Surely," everyone said, "we shall hear the bells now, for nothing like this has ever happened before!"

But still only the cold wind was heard in the tower, and people shook their heads and said they never really believed the story of the chimes and doubted if they had ever rung at all.

The procession was over, and the choir began the closing hymn. Suddenly the organist stopped playing and the old minister held his hand up for silence. As all the people strained to listen, there came softly, distinctly, swinging through the air, the sound of the chimes in the tower. So far away, and yet so clear the music seemed—so much sweeter than any sound they had ever heard before—that the people sat transfixed. Then they all stood up together and stared straight at the altar to see what great gift had awakened the long-silent bells.

But all that the nearest of them saw was the childish figure of Little Brother, who had crept softly down the aisle when no one was looking, and had laid Pedro's little piece of silver on the altar.

Christmas Among the Animals

Mary held her newborn baby in her arms. She was happy, but troubled too. It was cold in the stable, and there was a nasty draft. She pressed her little son against her heart and wished that her love could warm his cold little body.

Worried, she glanced at the big holes in the roof. Through the largest of these a beautiful flickering star looked down, the star which later was to show the way to the shepherds and the Three Magi. But Mary did not know about this yet. She was a mother, worried about her little baby, and waiting for Joseph, who had gone out to borrow some fire.

Tenderly cradling her little son in her arms, she looked around at the animals whose home she shared: an ox, a mule, a horse, a cow and a goat. It was obvious that the animals regarded her as an intruder, except perhaps for the ox: he looked friendly, sometimes glancing behind him to a corner where his sister, the cow, was giving birth to a little calf.

Mary was looking for a tiny place in which to put her son to sleep, but all she saw was the hard, rough ground, the heavy beams and dark corners full of spider webs. Maybe she could use the animals' manger. She filled it with some hay and laid down her baby. Then she tore off part of her dress to cover him and sat down quietly beside him.

The animals had been watching this for some time and the goat was working herself into a rage. Loudly bleating, she tried to set the others against the human beings. Such manners! Intruding upon their privacy, and taking their manger and their food too! Pretty soon the horse and the mule began to agree with the goat; they pounded the floor with their hoofs and cast mean looks at the little group of humans. Mary noticed it and felt the animals were justified. She got up and began to gather for them the hay which lay all over the stable floor. It was a difficult task but she felt that it was her duty, and finally she had assembled a whole lot of it.

But the big hungry horse thought that it wasn't enough. Full of contempt, he stamped his hoofs on the heap of hay, snorted indignantly, and tossed his mane in anger. What he wanted was that delicious bit of hay right under the little boy in the manger. He pushed the mule out of his way and began to nibble greedily.

Poor Mary was desperate. She took her baby in her arms again and began to pray. Suddenly she heard a sound on the roof, and when she looked up—lo!—there was a beautiful angel looking down at her through the biggest hole in the roof. He addressed the horse: "You greedy and intolerant animal! Henceforth you and your offspring shall serve and carry human beings. You are larger and more powerful than they are, but you will be their humble servant." And so it came to pass.

Meanwhile the ox felt sorry for Mary and her infant, and wanted to make up for what his friend had done. With his heavy hoofs he scraped some hay together for a bed and blew his warm breath comfortingly over the cold little baby. He had whispered in Mary's ear that his sister, the cow, wished to give her little calf to her son for a playmate.

Oh, how grateful was Mary! She looked up and—lo!—there was the angel again, this time peering at the ox through the biggest hole in the roof. "Henceforth," he said, "you and your sister shall eat in peace, and even digest your food four times. And your sister shall have a calf each year and always have plenty of milk." And so it came to pass.

The mule had listened to all these prophecies but didn't know whether to believe them or not. It was all rather silly, he thought. He had his own opinion and very bad manners. Suddenly he began to bray stupidly. When Mary was thanking the ox for his kindness, he snatched the hay away from under the baby and began to eat rapidly, while moving his long ears up and down.

But before Mary could do anything to prevent him—lo!—there was the angel shaking a menacing finger at the mule through the biggest hole in the roof. "Mule," he said, "just for this you and your kind will never have any babies as from this day." And so it came to pass.

One would think that this time the goat might have learned her lesson and behaved herself. But no, she was stupid and brazen. Still bleating loudly, she rushed through the stable, kicking up her heels and making a fool of herself. The little boy began to cry, and Mary didn't know what to do next. And when she looked up at the star shining through the roof—lo!—there was the angel sticking his head through the biggest hole. To this day the goat and her offspring have kept their silly laugh, and their milk has lost its good flavor, so that people don't like to drink it. And so it came to pass.

At long last, peace returned to the stable—wonderful, comforting peace. Joseph returned and brought some fire, the animals stood in awe, and a great and heavenly light shone through the biggest hole in the roof. The little infant fell into an untroubled sleep, and Mary folded her hands in prayer.

This is what happened during the holy night—at least, many people believe it, or at least that is what people in Holland tell one another.

Christmas Underground

from "A Wind in the Willows"

"What a capital little house this is!" Mr. Rat called out cheerily. "So compact! So well planned! Everything here and everything in its place! We'll make a jolly night of it. The first thing we want is a good fire; I'll see to that – I always know where to find things. So this is the parlour? Splendid! Your own idea, those little sleeping-bunks in the wall? Capital! Now, I'll fetch the wood and the coals, and you dust up a bit, Mole – bustle about, old chap!"

Encouraged by his merry companion, the Mole roused himself and, with energy and heartiness, dusted and polished the home from which he had so long been absent, while the Rat, running to and fro with armfuls of fuel, soon had a cheerful blaze roaring up the chimney . . .

Next they went and hunted through every cupboard, until they found a tin of sardines – a box of captain's biscuits, nearly full – and a German sausage encased in silver paper.

"There's a banquet for you!" observed the Rat, as he arranged the table. "I know some animals who would give their ears to be sitting down to supper with us tonight!"

"No bread!" groaned the Mole, "no butter, no –"

"No pate de foie gras, no champagne!" continued the Rat, grinning. "And that reminds me – what's that little door at the end of the passage? Your cellar, of course! Every luxury in this house! Just you wait a minute."

He made for the cellar door, and presently re-appeared, somewhat dusty, with a bottle of beer in each paw and another under each arm. "Self-indulgent beggar you seem to be, Mole," he observed. "Deny yourself nothing. This is really the jolliest little place I was ever in . . ."

Just as the Rat was getting seriously to work with the sardine-opener, sounds were heard from the forecourt without—sounds like the scuffling of small feet in the gravel and a confused murmur of tiny voices, while broken sentences reached them—"Now, all in a line—hold the lantern up a bit, Tommy—clear your throats first—no coughing after I say one, two, three—Where's young Bill?—Here, come on, do, we're all a-waiting—"

"What's up?" inquired the Rat, pausing in his labours.

"I think it must be the field-mice," replied the Mole, with a touch of pride in his manner. "They go round carol-singing regularly at this time of year. They're quite an institution in these parts. Before I left on my travels, they never passed me over—they always came to Mole End last of all; and I used to give them hot drinks, and supper sometimes . . . It will be like old times to hear them again!"

"Let's have a look at them!" cried the Rat, jumping up and running to the door.

It was a pretty sight, and a seasonable one, that met their eyes when they flung the door open. In the forecourt, lit by the dim rays of a horn lantern, a group of little field-mice stood in a semi-circle, red worsted comforters round their throats, their forepaws thrust deep into their pockets, their feet dancing for warmth. With bright beady eyes they glanced shyly at each other, sniggering a little, sniffing and applying coat-sleeves a great deal. As the door opened, one of the elder ones that carried a lantern was just saying, "Now then, one, two, three!" and forthwith their shrill little voices uprose on the air, singing one of the old-time carols that their forefathers composed in the fields that

were fallow and held by frost, or when snow-bound in chimney corners, and handed down to be sung in the miry street to lamp-lit windows at Yule-time.

> *Villagers all, this frosty tide,*
> *Let your doors swing open wide,*
> *Though wind may follow, and snow beside,*
> *Yet draw us in by your fire to bide;*
> *Joy shall be yours in the morning!*
>
> *Here we stand in the cold and the sleet,*
> *Blowing fingers and stamping feet,*
> *Come from far away you to greet—*
> *You by the fire and we in the street—*
> *Bidding you joy in the morning!*
>
> *For ere one half of the night was gone,*
> *Sudden a star had led us on,*
> *Raining bliss and benison—*
> *Bliss tomorrow and more anon,*
> *Joy for every morning!*
>
> *Goodman Joseph toiled through the snow—*
> *Saw the star o'er the stable low;*
> *Mary she might not further go—*
> *Welcome thatch, and litter below!*
> *Joy was hers in the morning!*
>
> *And when they heard the angels tell*
> *"Who were the first to cry Nowell?*
> *Animals all, as it befell,*
> *In the stable where they did dwell!"*
> *Joy shall be theirs in the morning!*

The voices ceased, the singers, bashful but smiling, exchanged sidelong glances, and silence succeeded—but for a moment only. Then, from up above and far away, the sound of distant bells rang a joyful and clangorous peal!

"Very well sung, boys!" cried the Rat heartily. "And now come along in, all of you, and warm yourselves by the fire, and have something hot!"

"Yes, come along, field-mice," cried Mole, eagerly. "This is quite like old times . . ."

In a very few minutes supper was ready, and Mole, as he took the head of the table, saw his little friends' faces brighten and beam as they fell to without delay; and he thought, "What a happy home-coming this has turned out to be, after all."

Yes, Virginia, There is a Santa Claus

As children grow older and wiser, parents inevitably are faced with the question, "Is there a Santa Claus?" When Virginia O'Hanlon asked that question of her parents in 1897, they suggested she write the NEW YORK SUN for an answer. She did, and Francis P. Church, a Civil War correspondent, wrote an editorial response which has become an American literary classic.

Dear Editor: I am 8 years old. Some of my little friends say there is no Santa Claus. Papa says "If you see it in The Sun it's so." Please tell me the truth. Is there a Santa Claus?

Virginia O'Hanlon

Virginia, your little friends are wrong. They have been affected by the skepticism of a skeptical age. They do not believe except they see. They think that nothing can be which is not comprehensible by their little minds. In this great universe of ours man is a mere insect, an ant, in his intellect, as compared with the boundless world about him, as measured by the intelligence capable of grasping the whole truth and knowledge.

Yes, Virginia, there is a Santa Claus. He exists as certainly as love and generosity and devotion exist, and you know that they abound and give to your life its highest beauty and joy. Alas! how dreary would be the world if there were no Santa Claus! It would be as dreary as if there were no Virginias. There would be no childlike faith then, no poetry, no romance to make tolerable this existence. We should have no enjoyment, except in the sense and sight. The eternal light with which childhood fills the world would be extinguished.

Not believe in Santa Claus! You might as well not believe in fairies! You might get your papa to hire men to watch all the chimneys on Christmas Eve to catch Santa Claus, but even if they did not see Santa Claus coming down what would that prove? The most real things in the world are those that neither children nor men can see. Did you ever see fairies dancing on the lawn? Of course not, but that's no proof that they are not there. Nobody can conceive or imagine all the wonders there are unseen and unseeable in the world.

You tear apart a baby's rattle and see what makes the noise inside, but there is a veil covering the unseen world which not the strongest men that ever lived could tear apart. Only faith, fancy, poetry, love, romance, can push aside that curtain and view and picture the supernal beauty and glory beyond. Is it all real? Ah, Virginia, in all this world there is nothing else real and abiding.

No Santa Claus? Thank God! he lives, and he lives forever. A thousand years from now, Virginia, nay, ten times ten thousand years from now, he will continue to make glad the heart of childhood.

A Very Murray Christmas

Murray wanted to run away. He was bored with his job as chief fluffy white stuffing stuffer at Santa's factory. He wanted adventure. And so, Murray planned his escape.

On Christmas Eve, when Murray was stuffing fluffy white stuffing into a brand new teddy bear, he left just enough room for himself to squeeze inside. Then, Murray sewed a secret zipper into the thick pile of the teddy bear's belly.

When the five o'clock whistle blew, Murray quickly slipped inside the teddy bear and zippered himself in, chuckling over his own cleverness all the while. When he heard Santa's "Ho, ho, ho," he sneaked open the zipper just enough to peek out.

"Time to load the stuffed toys into the sleigh," called out Santa. As soon as the jolly old elf had turned his back, Murray hopped his teddy bear to the front of the line.

Pretty soon Santa's sleigh was full and ready for takeoff. There was Murray perched on the top of a great pile of presents, his eager little eyes peering out into the wintry darkness. The reindeer pawed restlessly at the hard, snow-encrusted earth, waiting for the signal.

Murray gasped as he felt the sleigh suddenly shoot forward into the cold arctic sky. He was on his way!

Their first stop was in a small village nestled between two snow-capped mountains. Murray shivered. "I hope Santa doesn't leave me here," he thought. "It's much too cold."

The next stop was too cold, also, but the further they traveled, the warmer it became.

Now Murray was getting uncomfortable. "I hope Santa doesn't leave me here," he said. "It's much too hot."

They continued from house to house for a long time—houses with crackling fires and twinkling lights and the smell of gingerbread. Santa took soldiers and dolls, puzzles and books, from his big sack, but—much to Murray's dismay—he never chose Murray's bear.

"I'm probably going to end up right back at the North Pole," Murray sighed. "I did so want some adventure."

But finally, at the very last house, Santa took Murray's teddy bear by the ear and brought him down the chimney.

"Kerplop!"

Murray unzipped the zipper just enough to look around. There he was, tucked under a bright, tinseled tree with an angel on top. While Santa bustled about at his work, Murray quietly climbed out of his teddy bear. "Oh boy! Now for some real adventure!" he giggled.

Just as he was about to tiptoe up the stairs, he heard a noise.

"Hissss-growl—hisss!"

Murray's eyes opened wide as he stood face to face with a big yellow cat.

"Oh no!" cried Murray, as the cat swung a great sharp claw in his direction. "I wish Santa would come save me, but he doesn't even know I'm here!"

As the cat crept closer, Murray froze with fear. "I'm a goner!" he thought.

Just as the cat was about to pounce, Santa finished putting the last toy in place. "Ho, ho, ho—time to go!" he said.

The noise frightened the cat away. Murray let out a huge sigh of relief. "Saved!" he said to himself as he scurried back to the safety of his teddy bear.

Santa surveyed his work, then turned to go. But first he took Murray's teddy bear by the ear and carried him back up the chimney.

"Ho, ho, ho," he laughed as he started for home in his sleigh.

Murray was so thankful. "No more running away for me," he thought. "I want to go back where it's safe. Back where everyone knows me. Back home."

"Ho, ho, ho—" laughed Santa. "I know, I know."

Murray peeked out of the teddy bear right into Santa's kind, twinkling eyes.

"Oh, Santa, you knew I was in here all along!" exclaimed Murray.

"That I did!" Santa said, and then he laughed, "Merry Christmas, Murray . . . Merry Christmas!"

Grandma's Fast-Food
Christmas Dinner

Grandma was a cook. Some people are teachers, some are waitresses, but Grandma cooked. She would cook anything for any purpose. She cooked for relaxation, to vent her anger, to distract her from her worries and problems. Whatever she cooked was always good . . . sandwiches and fast foods were for novices according to the gospel by Grandma.

Preparing for a holiday, especially Christmas, always received Grandma's undivided attention. This particular Christmas was no exception. She was going all out. The children and grandchildren would all be at her house for Christmas dinner. Marlyn and Bob, with Betsy and

Wayne, would spend Christmas Eve with Grandma and Grandpa, but the others would arrive on Christmas morning.

Since five children and many friends had been served a lot of beautiful meals from Grandma's big old stove, Grandpa decided a new one would be a wonderful Christmas gift for her this year. It had to be equipped with all the modern conveniences such as timers and a self-cleaning oven. The stove arrived on Christmas Eve, so Grandma had very little time to read the instructions before putting it into service.

Christmas morning found the new stove at

work. There had to be plenty of desserts, including fancy candy and cookies. With a full dozen around that beautiful dinner table, a lot of food had to be prepared before two o'clock rolled around and the rest of the family arrived.

Betsy and Wayne were like all children; they were interested in what was going on in the kitchen. Betsy helped by peeling the potatoes and Wayne chopped the onions for the turkey stuffing, his tears mixing in with the seasoning. Everything was going right on schedule.

"Isn't that a heart-warming sight in the kitchen?" Marlyn asked Bob.

"And how about that gorgeous table. I'm hungry just looking at it," Bob responded.

As the other family members arrived, Grandma took one more look in the new oven at the roasting turkey, basting it and taking a deep, long smell of its wonderful aroma. "Time to put in the yams and rolls," Grandma said to herself. "Everything's finishing up just fine!"

"Betsy, sprinkle the top of the yams with marshmallows and put them in with the other things," Grandma directed. "They just need a minute to melt." Betsy was elated at the idea of having such an important job, so she did it quickly. In went the yams. Then Betsy closed the door firmly and, just to make sure everything was secure, she pushed the lever marked L-O-C-K.

"Everything's in the oven, Grandma," Betsy said proudly. "I even locked the door to keep things safe and sound!"

Just then Grandma remembered reading something in the instructions about locking the door to clean the oven . . . and how, for safety purposes, the oven could not be unlocked until the temperature had cooled down.

Sure enough, Grandma was exactly right. Inside the safely locked oven were the turkey, stuffing, yams with marshmallows and those delicious homemade dinner rolls Grandma had made—all ready to be eaten. After an hour or so of fruitless tries by every one of those twelve hungry people to unlock the door, the oven was still locked.

So Grandma picked up the telephone, called a fast-food driveby, and ordered twelve burgers with fries. "They must be on individual plates," Grandma said. "Someone will be by to get them right away."

As everyone found their places at the elegantly set table, they looked at the fancy gelatin salads, cranberries, desserts, holiday punch . . . and twelve bountifully filled paper plates!

When young Wayne was asked to give thanks for the dinner, he even remembered to thank God for the hamburgers! After all, it's who you are sharing Christmas with that really matters, not what you have to eat.

The Gift of the Magi

One dollar and eighty-seven cents. That was all. And sixty cents of it was in pennies, saved one and two at a time. Three times Della counted it. One dollar and eighty-seven cents. And tomorrow was Christmas.

There was nothing to do but flop down on the shabby little couch and sob. So Della did.

While the mistress of the house is giving way to this display of emotion, let's take a look at the home. A modest, furnished flat at $8 per week. In the entryway was a letter box into which no letter would fit, and an electric button which would not ring. Beneath it was a card bearing the name "Mr. James Dillingham Young." And though the proud possessor of this name boasted a weekly income of but $20 a week, whenever he came home, he was called "Jim" and greatly hugged by Mrs. James Dillingham Young, already introduced to you as Della. Which is all very good.

Della finished her cry and attended to her cheeks with a powder rag. She stood by the window and looked out dully at a gray cat walking a gray fence in a gray backyard. Tomorrow was Christmas Day, and she had only $1.87 with which to buy Jim a present. She had been saving for months, and this was the result. Only $1.87 to buy a gift for Jim. Many a happy hour she had spent planning something nice for him—something fine and rare.

Suddenly she whirled from the window and stood before the mirror. Her eyes were shining brilliantly, but her face had lost its color. Rapidly she pulled down her long, full hair.

There were two possessions of the James Dillingham Youngs in which they both took pride. One was Jim's gold watch, which had been his father's and his grandfather's. The other was Della's hair.

Now Della's hair cascaded down to her knees like a shining brown waterfall. Then she did it up nervously and quickly, faltering only for a minute to wipe away a tear.

On went her old brown jacket and hat, and with a whirl of her skirts and the sparkle still in her eyes, she fluttered out the door and down to the street. Where she stopped, the sign read, "Mme. Sofronie, Hair Goods of All Kind." One flight up Della ran and collected herself. Madame, large, too white, chilly, hardly looked the "Sofronie."

"Will you buy my hair?" asked Della.

"Take off your hat and let's have a look at it," said Madame.

Down rippled the brown cascade. "Twenty dollars," said Madame, lifting the mass with a practiced hand.

"Give it to me quick," said Della.

The next two hours flew by as Della ransacked the stores for Jim's present. She found it at last. It was a golden fob chain—so elegant, so good, it was even worthy of Jim's watch. As soon as she saw it she knew it must be his. Quietness and value—the description applied to both. Twenty-one dollars at cost, and she hurried home with 87 cents.

When Della reached home, her intoxication gave way to reason. She got out her curling irons and within forty minutes, her head was covered with tiny curls that made her look wonderfully like a truant schoolboy.

At 7 o'clock, the coffee was brewing and the stove was ready for the pork chops. Jim was never late. Della doubled the precious fob chain in her hand and waited by the door. When she heard his step, she went white for a moment. "Please, God," she whispered, "make him think I'm still pretty."

The door opened and in stepped Jim. He looked thin and very serious for one so young, and he needed a new overcoat.

He stopped inside the door, immovable, his eyes fixed on Della in an expression she could not read.

"Jim, darling," she cried, "don't look at me that way. I had my hair cut off and sold it because I couldn't live through Christmas without giving you a present. It'll grow out again. My hair grows awfully fast. Say 'Merry Christmas' and let's be happy. You don't know what a nice — what a beautiful, nice gift I've got for you."

"You've cut off your hair?" asked Jim, laboriously.

"Yes," said Della. "Don't you like me just as well? I'm still me without my hair, aren't I?"

"You say your hair is gone?" he said, with an air almost of idiocy.

"You needn't look for it," said Della. "It's sold—sold and gone. It's Christmas Eve. Be good to me, for it went for you."

Out of his trance Jim seemed quickly to wake. He hugged Della tightly. Then he drew a package from his overcoat pocket and threw it upon the table.

"Don't make any mistake, Della," he said, "about me. I don't think there's anything that could make me like my girl less. But if you'll unwrap that package, you'll see why you had me going at first."

White fingers tore at the string and paper. And then a scream of joy followed quickly by a flood of tears.

For there lay The Combs—the set of combs Della had worshipped for so long in a Broadway window. Beautiful, tortoise shell combs with jewelled rims—just the shade to wear in the beautiful vanished hair. They were expensive, and her heart had yearned for them without the least hope of possession. Now they were hers, but the tresses they were to have adorned were gone.

But she hugged them to her, and at length she was able to look up with a tearful smile and say, "My hair grows so fast, Jim!"

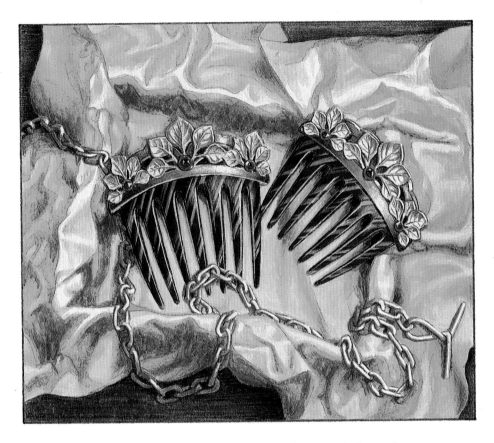

Then Della leaped up and eagerly held out Jim's fine gift upon her open palm. The dull precious metal seemed to flash with a reflection of her bright ardent spirit.

"Isn't it dandy, Jim? I hunted all over town for it. You'll have to check the time a hundred times a day now. Give me your watch so I can see how it looks."

Instead, Jim tumbled onto the couch and smiled.

"Della," he said, "let's put our Christmas presents away and keep 'em awhile. They're too nice to use just at present. I sold the watch to buy your combs. And now suppose we put those chops on."

The magi, as you know, were wonderfully wise men who brought gifts to the Babe in the manger. They invented the art of giving presents. Being wise, their gifts were no doubt wise ones. And here I have lamely related the tale of two foolish children who most unwisely sacrificed for each other the greatest treasures of their house. But in a last word to the wise, let it be said that of all who give gifts, these two were the wisest. Of all who give and receive gifts, such as they are the wisest. Everywhere they are wisest. They are the magi.

Christmas Bells

Written in 1863, this poem expresses Henry Wadsworth Longfellow's feelings upon hearing the Christmas bells at a time when the Civil War raged and his son lay seriously wounded from the fighting. Though "Christmas Bells" has since become a Christmas carol, it is also a poem about war and peace.

I heard the bells on Christmas Day
Their old, familiar carols play,
   And wild and sweet
   The words repeat
Of peace on earth, good-will to men!

And thought how, as the day had come,
The belfries of all Christendom
   Had rolled along
   The unbroken song
Of peace on earth, good-will to men!

Till, ringing, swinging on its way,
The world revolved from night to day
   A voice, a chime,
   A chant sublime
Of peace on earth, good-will to men!

Then from each black, accursed mouth
The cannon thundered in the South
    And with the sound
    The carols drowned
Of peace on earth, good-will to men!

It was as if an earthquake rent
The hearth-stones of a continent,
    And made forlorn
    The households born
Of peace on earth, good-will to men!

And in despair I bowed my head;
"There is no peace on earth," I said;
    "For hate is strong
    And mocks the song
Of peace on earth, good-will to men!"

Then pealed the bells more loud and deep,
"God is not dead; nor doth He sleep!
    The Wrong shall fail,
    The Right prevail,
With peace on earth, good-will to men!"

How Saint Francis Told the Christmas Story

The Italian sunshine was warm and bright as Saint Francis walked in the woods near the village of Greccio. The year was 1223 and the month December.

Saint Francis moved slowly, head bowed. "It's almost here, Il Natale, the birth of Jesus, the season of good will. But the people here in Greccio seem to have forgotten Jesus. They constantly hurt each other by their cruel and selfish ways. If only I could help them think about that first Christmas night and about the baby Jesus, who, when he became a man, 'went about doing good.'"

Saint Francis continued to ponder as he walked. Then he stopped suddenly, a light glowing in his eyes. "I know! I know what I can do!"

With that he quickened his steps until he reached the home of his friend, Giovanni, to whom he unfolded his plan. Giovanni was enthusiastic too.

If you had been in the Greccio Woods the next afternoon, you would have seen a procession of Giovanni's servants making their way to the big cave. Some carried boughs of pine and cypress, others lumber and a bale of straw. Two more brought from Giovanni's stable a manger filled with hay. A neighboring farmer arrived with three white cows, sheep, and lambs.

Meanwhile, word had spread around the village that Saint Francis was inviting everyone to come to the cave that night.

When it grew dark, men, women, and chil-

dren approached the cave, bearing torches and candles. Upon entering, they stood transfixed with awe and wonder. There, before their very eyes they *saw* the Christmas story—the stable spread with clean straw and the walls covered with sweet-smelling greens. The white cows chewed their cud, and a little gray donkey looked quietly into the hay-filled manger, while sheep and lambs crouched close.

At the appointed time, a young father and mother came forward and gently laid their sleeping baby in the manger. When the picture was thus completed, Saint Francis stepped from the shadowed corner where he had been standing.

Looking into the faces of the hushed and reverent worshipers, he told the Bethlehem story of Mary and Joseph, of the shepherds and the Wise Men. He spoke not only of the baby Jesus, but also of Jesus, the man, and implored his listeners to follow Jesus' way of loving-kindness.

Later that evening when the villagers left the cave to return to their homes, the winter stars were shining brightly in the dark sky.

"See!" exclaimed a child, pointing to one star which was especially large and bright. "It's the star of Bethlehem!"

Saint Francis heard it and his heart sang with joy. He knew that Christmas—the real Christmas—had come that night to the village of Greccio, Italy.

Santa Gets the Bug

It was that time of year again! Santa went out to the barn to make sure everything was in order for the long trip ahead. Spirit, his trusty old sleigh, sat napping in the corner as Santa walked around him, scratching his chin.

"Well," thought Santa, "his paint is peeling a bit and — my, oh, my — look how rusty his runners have gotten." The harness for the reindeer was certainly showing signs of wear and tear, and just where Santa sat there was a big rip in the upholstery. "Ho-hum. Better call a few elves to help out," mused Santa as he made his way back to the house.

Santa had just settled into his great, overstuffed easy chair when Mrs. Claus turned on the TV. There on the local North Pole station was Friendly Alf the Elf decked out in his bright red suit coat.

"Tired of that rickety old sleigh? Want something with splash, with dash—but for not much cash?! Then come on down to Friendly Alf's New and Used Sleigh Lot! Trade-ins welcome!"

"How silly," remarked Mrs. Claus. "Always thinking new is better than tried and true."

She shook her head and changed channels, but it was too late. Santa's eyes were wide and bright; his cheeks were flushed with excitement. He had been bitten by the new sleigh bug!

Wouldn't it be fun to have a shiny new sleigh, he thought. Why, he had friends who traded their sleighs in every year for the latest model while he'd had *his* sleigh for centuries!

Santa stole a sidelong glance at Mrs. Claus as she sat knitting. She'd never understand. Better not mention it to her and then surprise her with it. When she saw how stylish and sleek the new sleigh would be, she'd have to admit he was right.

First thing the next morning Santa went over to pay Friendly Alf a visit.

"Why Santa—welcome to the 20th century! Finally decided to get yourself some new wheels—or runners, as the case may be? Har, har!" welcomed Alf.

"Now, now!" said Santa. "I'm just shopping around. Thought I'd see what you have to offer."

"Have I got a deal for you, Santa!" Alf enthused as he led Santa Claus to a spiffy new compact sleigh. "Now I know you're thinking 'looks mighty small,' but don't let looks be deceiving! This little hummer can hold as much as your old sleigh and more!"

Santa found this a little hard to believe. Alf continued, "She's a snap to park and, best of all, she only needs four reindeer to get the same mileage you get now with eight! Course you might have to stop and feed them a little more often, but what the hay! Har, har—get it, what the . . ."

Santa smiled kindly and said, "I don't think so, Alf. My toys couldn't possibly all fit."

"Do not despair," said Alf as he led Santa to a large, luxury model. "This baby was just made for you—lots of chrome, carols in quadriphonic sound—power 'deering' on everything! And check out this mirror. Never know when that beard might need a little trim!"

Santa settled into one of the deep soft leather cushions and leaned back his head. "Z-z-z-z-z-z-."

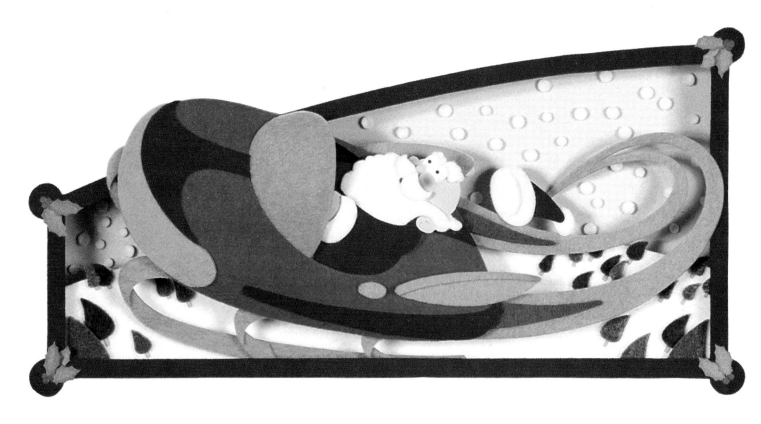

"Hey, Santa—wake up, old buddy. Pretty comfy, eh?" Santa heard Alf's voice say through a haze.

"This will never do! I have to stay wide awake during my long journey!"

"Okay, Santa—I don't show this next model to just anyone. They're usually on back order for months, but I just happen to have a demo available."

With a flourish, Alf presented to Santa the latest thing in sports sleighs. "Faster than a rocket, a racing stripe in the color of your choice, got an engine with 2000 reindeer power. It'll lay a streak of chrome like you've never seen!"

Santa was impressed. "What kind of ride does she have?"

"Slick as a whistle—or the down on a thistle, as the case may be. Har, har! Go ahead—take her for a spin!" Alf urged.

Cautiously Santa lowered himself into the driver's compartment and stepped on the gas pedal. The sleigh jerked up into the sky like a shot, snapping Santa's head back so that his red furry hat went flying into the air. Only the echo of Santa's voice yelling "Wh-o-a-a" remained behind. Shortly Santa brought her blasting back in for a landing and climbed down, a bit weak in the knees.

"Oops! A little whiplash there, old pal?" asked Alf with a little look of concern on his elfin face.

"Oh, I'm fine," answered Santa. "It was 'interesting,' Alf, but just not my speed, so to speak."

So Alf showed Santa more sleighs—blue ones, green ones, ones

P. FICKLING

with white-wall runners and tape decks and map lights. Finally Santa
climbed into one that felt just right. The dashboard gleamed with bright
chrome and deeply polished wood. The seat was soft and comfortable
and smelled of pine and new-fallen snow. It was just the right size. Of
course, the runners were rusty and the paint was peeling just a bit.

"How much is this one?" inquired Santa. Alf just looked at him and
smiled.

"Oh, Santa—you just sleigh me. Har, har. That's the one you CAME
in!" Alf hadn't had this much fun *not* making a sale in years and years.

"Ho, ho! By george, you're right," chuckled Santa, a bit embarrassed.
"Shame on me! Ho, ho, ho!" Alf just shook his head and waved as Santa
pulled out of the used sleigh lot in his trusty old companion, Spirit.

Mrs. Claus was waiting at the door with a plate of freshly baked
cookies. "Where've you been all day, Dear?"

"Oh, just trying to recapture my lost youth," Santa smiled as he
sampled a cookie. "This is good! Did you really use that mix in a box?"

"I tried it for the first batch," Mrs. Claus answered, "but it just
didn't taste the same. So I threw them out and started over with my
old recipe."

Santa chuckled to himself. He gave Mrs. Claus a peck on the cheek,
and said, "Yes, sometimes the old way is the best way." Mrs. Claus smiled
knowingly as they walked arm-in-arm into their snug, warm little cottage.

Outside the new snow fell softly and silently down upon their little
roof. And inside the closed up barn, Spirit's runners shone in the safe,
still darkness, like comets streaking silver across the night sky.

The Holy Night

It was a Christmas Day and all the folks had driven to church except Grandmother and I. I believe we were all alone in the house. We had not been permitted to go along, because one of us was too old and the other was too young. And we were sad, both of us, because we had not been taken to early mass to hear the singing and to see the Christmas candles.

But as we sat there in our loneliness, Grandmother began to tell a story.

"There was a man," said she, "who went out in the dark night to borrow live coals to kindle a fire. He went from hut to hut and knocked.

'Dear friends, help me!' said he. 'My wife has just given birth to a child, and I must make a fire to warm her and the little one.'

"But it was way in the night, and all the people were asleep. No one replied.

"The man walked and walked. At last he saw the gleam of a fire a long way off. Then he went in that direction, and saw that the fire was burning in the open. A lot of sheep were sleeping around the fire, and an old shepherd sat and watched over the flock.

"When the man who wanted to borrow fire came up to the sheep, he saw that three big dogs lay asleep at the shepherd's feet. All three awoke when the man approached and opened their great jaws, as though they wanted to bark; but not a sound was heard. The man noticed that the hair on their backs stood up and that their sharp, white teeth glistened in the firelight. They dashed toward him. He felt that one of them bit at his leg and one at his hand and that one clung to his throat. But their jaws and teeth wouldn't obey them, and the man didn't suffer the least harm.

"Now the man wished to go farther, to get what he needed. But the sheep lay back to back and so close to one another that he couldn't pass them. Then the man stepped on their backs and walked over them and up to the fire. And not one of the animals awoke or moved."

Thus far, Grandmother had been allowed to narrate without interruption. But at this point I couldn't help breaking in. "Why didn't they do it, Grandma?" I asked.

"That you shall hear in a moment," said Grandmother—and went on with her story.

"When the man had almost reached the fire, the shepherd looked up. He was a surly old man, who was unfriendly and harsh toward human beings. And when he saw the strange man coming, he seized the long spiked staff, which he always held in his hand when he tended his flock, and threw it at him. The staff came right toward the man, but before it reached him, it turned off to one side and whizzed past him far out in the meadow."

When Grandmother had got this far, I interrupted her again. "Grandma, why wouldn't the stick hurt the man?" Grandmother did not bother about answering me, but continued her story.

"Now the man came up to the shepherd and said to him: 'Good man, help me, and lend me a little fire! My wife has just given birth to a child, and I must make a fire to warm her and the little one.'

"The shepherd would rather have said no, but when he pondered that the dogs couldn't hurt the man, and the sheep had not run from him, and that the staff had not wished to strike him, he was a little afraid, and dared not deny the man that which he asked.

"'Take as much as you need!' he said to the man.

"But then the fire was nearly burnt out. There were no logs or branches left, only a big heap of live coals; and the stranger had neither spade nor shovel, wherein he could carry the red-hot coals.

"When the shepherd saw this, he said again: 'Take as much as you need!' And he was glad that the man wouldn't be able to take away any coals.

"But the man stooped and picked coals from the ashes with his bare hands, and laid them in his mantle. And he didn't burn his hands when he touched them, nor did the coals scorch his mantle; but he carried them away as if they had been nuts or apples."

But here the story-teller was interrupted for the third time. "Grandma, why wouldn't the coals burn the man?"

"That you shall hear," said Grandmother, and went on:

"And when the shepherd, who was such a cruel and hard-hearted man, saw all this, he began to wonder to himself: 'What kind of a night is this, when the dogs do not bite, the sheep are not scared, the staff does not kill, or the fire scorch?' He called the stranger back, and said to him: 'What kind of a night is this? And how does it happen that all things show you compassion?'

"Then said the man: 'I cannot tell you if you yourself do not see it.' And he wished to go his way, that he might soon make a fire and warm his wife and child.

"But the shepherd did not wish to lose sight of the man before he had found out what all this might portend. He got up and followed the man till they came to the place where he lived.

"Then the shepherd saw that the man didn't have so much as a hut to dwell in, but that his wife and babe were lying in a mountain cave, where there was nothing except the cold and naked stone walls.

"But the shepherd thought that perhaps the poor innocent child might freeze to death there in the cave; and, although he was a hard man, he was touched, and thought he would like to help it. And he loosened his knapsack from his shoulder, took from it a soft white sheepskin, gave it to the strange man, and said that he should let the child sleep on it.

"But just as soon as he showed that he, too, could be merciful, his eyes were opened, and he saw what he had not been able to see before and heard what he could not have heard before.

"He saw that all around him stood a ring of little silver-winged angels, and each held a stringed instrument, and all sang in loud tones that tonight the Saviour was born who should redeem the world from its sins.

"Then he understood how all things were so happy this night that they didn't want to do anything wrong.

"And it was not only around the shepherd that there were angels, but he saw them everywhere. They sat inside the cave, they sat outside on the mountain, and they flew under the heavens. They came marching in great companies, and, as they passed, they paused and cast a glance at the child.

"There were such jubilation and such gladness and songs and play. And all this he saw in the dark night, whereas before he could not have made out anything. He was so happy because his eyes had been opened that he fell upon his knees and thanked God."

Here Grandmother sighed and said: "What that shepherd saw we might also see, for the angels fly down from heaven every Christmas Eve, if we could only see them."

Then Grandmother laid her hand on my head, and said: "You must remember this, for it is as true, as true as that I see you and you see me. It is not revealed by the light of lamps or candles, and it does not depend upon sun and moon; but that which is needful is, that we have such eyes as can see God's glory."

The Christmas Story

Long ago in the city of Nazareth a story began which we still remember today, for it is the story about the true meaning of Christmas.

A young woman named Mary lived in Nazareth then, and she had such a miraculous thing happen to her that we bless her name still. One day while she was sitting at home an angel of God appeared to her. Mary had never seen an angel before and she was very afraid until God's angel, seeing how frightened Mary was, spoke to her in a reassuring voice.

"Fear not, Mary," the angel said. "For thou hast found favor with God. And behold, thou shalt conceive in thy womb and bring forth a son, and shalt call his name Jesus."

Then the angel explained to Mary that the baby which would be born to her would be the promised Messiah, the Son of God.

Mary was very glad to be so honored by God and was eager to give birth to Jesus, yet she wondered how God could make this happen since she was not yet married to Joseph, the carpenter she loved. She knew all babies must have both a father and a mother. However, the angel told her that the Holy Spirit would descend upon her to make this miracle happen, and Mary knew it would be as the angel had said.

The Bible tells us that Joseph, too, was visited by an angel. This angel came to him in a dream and explained to him that the baby growing inside of Mary was the baby Jesus, the Son of God. Joseph was honored to make Mary his wife and to share in her excitement as they waited for Jesus to be born.

In those days the Roman Emperor, Caesar

Augustus, ruled most of the known world. He ruled very sternly, and his soldiers were both feared and hated for they were swift to punish anyone who did not obey Caesar. Therefore, when a decree went out from Caesar ordering everyone to return to their native cities to be taxed and counted, Joseph knew he would have to obey.

As a descendent of David, Joseph had to return to Bethlehem to obey Caesar's order. He knew it would be a long journey for Mary, who the Bible tells us was "great with child." However, he couldn't bear to leave Mary behind when the birth was so near, so with Joseph leading the donkey on which Mary rode, they traveled from Nazareth in the Province of Galilee into Judea to Bethlehem, the City of David. It was a long trip. It was several days later when they finally reached Bethlehem, and Mary was very tired from the journey.

As they entered the walls of the city they realized that many people had arrived before them. The streets were very crowded and the people jostled Mary as Joseph led them from inn to inn in an effort to find a room. Unfortunately, all the inns were full. Finally, one innkeeper, seeing how very tired Mary was, took pity on them and welcomed them to spend the night in the stable behind the inn. When Mary saw the warm barn full of sweet smelling hay and the friendly faces of the stable animals, God's creatures all, she surely knew this would be a good place for the Christ child to be born.

And so, as the Bible tells us, she "brought forth her firstborn son, and wrapped him in swaddling clothes and laid him in a manger."

Lined with soft, warm hay, it made a perfect little bed for the baby Jesus.

How proud Mary and Joseph must have felt as they looked down on their son that night, for they knew he was also God's Son, and that he would bring so much peace to the world. They knew that God must also be feeling proud, but they didn't know that at that very moment God was sending messengers from heaven to tell the world of the baby's birth.

In the same country, a group of shepherds were keeping watch over their flocks of sheep on the night Jesus was born. Imagine their surprise when, all of a sudden, the whole sky seemed to glow with a brilliant light and an angel of God appeared! Just as Mary had been afraid when the angel had visited her in Nazareth, the shepherds were very afraid and they fell to their knees. But their fright was soon replaced with joy when they heard the angel speak.

"Fear not," the angel said. "For behold, I bring you good tidings of great joy, which shall be to all people. For unto you is born this day in the city of David a Saviour, which is Christ the Lord. And this shall be a sign unto you; ye shall find the babe wrapped in swaddling clothes, lying in a manger."

And as the angel spoke, suddenly more angels filled the sky, a multitude of heavenly host praising God and saying, "Glory to God in the highest and on earth peace, good will toward men."

As soon as the angels departed, the shepherds excitedly made plans to journey to Bethlehem where they could "see this thing which has come to pass, which the Lord has made known to us." When they arrived they found Mary and Joseph, and the babe lying in the manger, and they knelt down and gave thanks that God had blessed them so.

After the shepherds left Bethlehem, they spread the good news of Jesus' birth to everyone they saw because they were filled with so much love and adoration.

Yet they were not the only ones who came to see the baby Jesus in Bethlehem. For in addition to sending the heavenly angels to announce the birth to the shepherds, God sent another message in the form of a brilliant star. The star was seen by three wise men in the East, who some say were astrologers. Watching the heavens, they became fascinated by the new star and came to Jerusalem to inquire, "Where is he that is born King of the Jews? For we have seen his star in the East, and are come to worship him."

From Jerusalem the three wise men, whom tradition tells us were named Casper, Balthazar and Melchior, followed the star of Bethlehem until it came to rest above the stable where Jesus was. Upon seeing the baby in Mary's arms, they fell down before Him and worshipped Him and they laid before Him gifts of gold, frankincense and myrrh—the richest gifts of the day.

As God's son, Jesus played and dreamed as all young boys do, but also knew he had his Father's work to do on earth. As a man, he travelled throughout the Holy Land healing the sick, saving the souls of those who had sinned and telling all people of God's will and of his love for them. When Jesus had finished his work on earth, he was crucified on the cross and died. But he arose from the grave three days later and went to live with his Father in heaven. We celebrate Jesus' resurrection on Easter Sunday. We celebrate his birth on Christmas.

Christmas will always include Santa Claus, electric trains, an orange in the toe of a stocking and visions of sugar plums. It will always be a time to rejoice together and let the Christmas spirit fill our hearts. But most of all, Christmas will always be a time for celebrating the birth of Jesus Christ. God's gift to us on that first Christmas Day was the greatest gift of all.

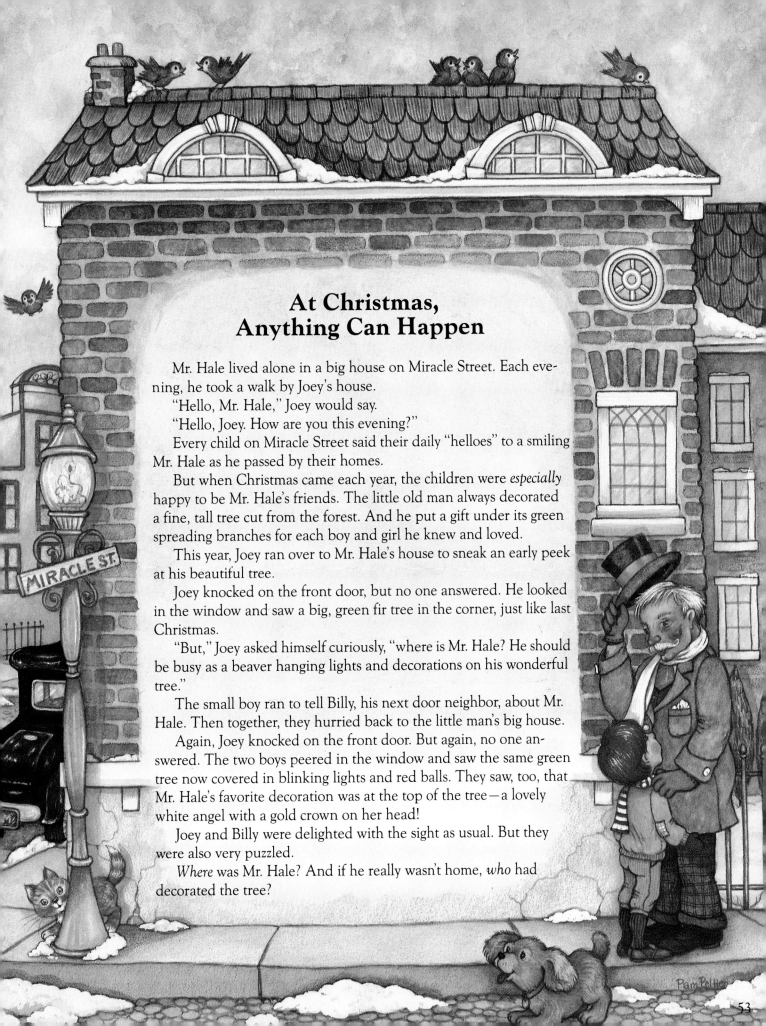

At Christmas,
Anything Can Happen

Mr. Hale lived alone in a big house on Miracle Street. Each evening, he took a walk by Joey's house.

"Hello, Mr. Hale," Joey would say.

"Hello, Joey. How are you this evening?"

Every child on Miracle Street said their daily "helloes" to a smiling Mr. Hale as he passed by their homes.

But when Christmas came each year, the children were *especially* happy to be Mr. Hale's friends. The little old man always decorated a fine, tall tree cut from the forest. And he put a gift under its green spreading branches for each boy and girl he knew and loved.

This year, Joey ran over to Mr. Hale's house to sneak an early peek at his beautiful tree.

Joey knocked on the front door, but no one answered. He looked in the window and saw a big, green fir tree in the corner, just like last Christmas.

"But," Joey asked himself curiously, "where is Mr. Hale? He should be busy as a beaver hanging lights and decorations on his wonderful tree."

The small boy ran to tell Billy, his next door neighbor, about Mr. Hale. Then together, they hurried back to the little man's big house.

Again, Joey knocked on the front door. But again, no one answered. The two boys peered in the window and saw the same green tree now covered in blinking lights and red balls. They saw, too, that Mr. Hale's favorite decoration was at the top of the tree — a lovely white angel with a gold crown on her head!

Joey and Billy were delighted with the sight as usual. But they were also very puzzled.

Where was Mr. Hale? And if he really wasn't home, *who* had decorated the tree?

53

The two boys ran down the street to tell their other friends about the mystery. And all together, they raced back to Mr. Hale's house.

Joey knocked on the front door, this time as loudly as he could—loud enough to wake a herd of sleeping elephants. Still, no one answered. All the children looked in the window and saw the beautiful tree that was now encircled by brightly wrapped gifts.

"Mr. Hale *must* be home!" Joey declared, full of worry. "He might be sick." And when he went up to the front door, it opened all by itself.

The children dashed inside! They searched for Mr. Hale in every room on the first floor of the big house, but found no one. They were about to go upstairs to look, when they heard a slight noise coming from the stairway. They turned to see a beautiful lady dressed in white, with a gold crown on her head, carrying more colorfully wrapped packages.

"Oh, there you all are!" she exclaimed joyfully. "I was afraid you wouldn't come. My brother, Mr. Hale, would have been *so* disappointed if you hadn't."

"Where is our friend?" Joey asked with deep concern.

"Yes, where is he?" asked Billy and all the others.

The lovely lady put down the presents and spoke softly to the children. "Well, Mr. Hale is in the hospital for a while because he hurt his back. And I thought, how wonderful it would be if perhaps I prepared everything just the way he does every Christmas Eve."

Then the lady in white, who reminded Joey of someone special, gave each child a gift to be opened on Christmas morning. Afterwards, she served ice cream piled high on pink cones and chocolate cake! Just as Mr. Hale would have done.

Later they sang carols and wished each other, as very good friends do, a merry Christmas.

Still, Joey felt an emptiness inside—without Mr. Hale to share in the party. "If Mr. Hale knew we have such nice presents, he would be happy, too, and get well sooner," Joey said to his friends. "Let's go tell Mr. Hale about the beautiful tree and everything!"

Just before the children waved goodbye to Mr. Hale's sister, she took down the angel from the top of the tree and gave it to Joey.

At the hospital, Mr. Hale's sad face brightened at the sight of the children, his friends. He sat up in bed. "I'm sorry I couldn't put up a tree this Christmas, kiddies," he said. "Or give you ice cream and cake and lovely presents."

Joey laid his hand on Mr. Hale's shoulder. "Don't worry. Your sister took care of everything. This Christmas Eve was just the same as always, except we missed you. Your sister is a wonderful lady."

Joey was still holding the angel given to him from the top of Mr. Hale's Christmas tree. And suddenly, he remembered who the kind lady in white reminded him of. "See, Mr. Hale—your sister looked exactly like this angel!"

Mr. Hale's face went pale, but a twinkle came in his eye. "Why, Joey, that can't be! My only sister went to heaven years ago," he sighed.

Joey stared deeply into the face of the angel in his hand and noticed something very strange—something *very strange* indeed. "Mr. Hale," he said in a soft, wondering voice, "I don't think your angel was smiling last Christmas. No, I'm sure she wasn't smiling last year."

"So, *why*," Joey asked, "is she smiling *now?*"

Mr. Hale took hold of the dainty little figure in white and stared into its tiny face. A big smile appeared on the old man's face, too. "You know, Joey, I think you're right," he said. "I can't remember the angel smiling when my sister gave it to me years ago."

"But after all," Mr. Hale continued, his blue eyes growing moist, "I suppose at Christmas anything can happen on Miracle Street."

Joey moved closer to Mr. Hale's bed and put his arms around his neck. What a strange, mysterious, *wonderful* Christmas Eve this had been . . .

55

Christmas is for Children

Christmas is for children—
　　at least that's what they say.
It's a time of wide-eyed wonder,
　　a magic holiday
When candy canes and gingerbread
　　fill tummies with delight
And little sleepyheads try hard
　　to stay up through the night.
Yes, Christmas is for children—
　　anyone will tell you so.
The twinkling, colored lights on trees
　　make youngsters' eyes just glow!
Each package and each stocking
　　is approached with childish joy
And toys bring squeals of laughter
　　from each eager girl and boy.
Yes, Christmas is for children—
　　all they say is true.
How wonderful that at Christmas time—
　　grownups are children, too!

The Christmas Cuckoo

Christkind means "Christ Child" in German. Originally it was the name given the holy infant, Jesus, who was thought to bring gifts for children. Eventually, the name evolved to represent a veiled, angelic helper, with a flowing white robe and golden wings, who brings the gifts on Christmas Eve. The Christkind is anxiously awaited each year in certain areas of Switzerland, Austria, Germany and in the Pennsylvania Dutch country of the United States.

nce upon a time in a tiny village deep in a mountain valley, there lived a lovely cuckoo. Oh, he was not a real cuckoo—not the kind that goes flitting gaily through flowered meadows and still forests. No . . . he was a wooden cuckoo and lived in a beautifully carved cuckoo clock which hung high on the parlor wall of a pretty house in a tiny little village.

Of course, he had not always lived there. He had been born deep in the Black Forest in a clockmaker's cottage. That had been a wonderful place to live! The walls were lined with rows of cuckoo clocks, and the little wooden birds spent their days happily singing out the hours to each other. Some of the cuckoos were even lucky enough to share their clocks with delicately carved quails with whom they took turns calling out the hour and half hour. Some clocks had chimes, others wooden couples who danced the quadrille; one even had a fraulein who promenaded in a painted garden and kissed her sweetheart every quarter hour.

The cuckoo was proud indeed of his clock home with its delicately carved birds and leaves and its painted bands of hearts and flowers. Beneath his doorway was a balcony with four wooden soldiers who circled continuously as the pendulum swung to and fro. But what made his house most special was a large reindeer head carved at the peak of the roof.

Having been carved by the clockmaker in the summer, the cuckoo had really never experienced Christmas. He had heard of it, of course. From the time the first crimson leaf dropped at summer's end, the older cuckoos talked of nothing else. They told of the tinkling music boxes which then lay half assembled on the clockmaker's workbench. They told of fir trees resplendent with marzipan fruit and silver nuts. Especially they told of the Christkind who magically appeared bearing gifts on Christmas Eve.

However, long before Christmas came, the little cuckoo's clock was packed in a box of fragrant pine chips and journeyed far to live with the family in the pretty house in the tiny village. At first it was fun to hang on the wall of such an elegant parlor and to be admired by four beaming children. They danced and clapped whenever he announced the hours, but after several days they began to tire of him. As time passed, he grew sad and lonely. He felt tired and no longer sang out the hours as cheerfully. "Perhaps," thought the cuckoo, "when Christmas comes they will begin to notice me again." And he began to look for signs of Christmas.

One day, when he came out at noontime, he noticed the eldest girl cutting gingerbread men with a sharp knife while the younger children pressed currants into the dough for eyes and buttons. The following day an advent wreath appeared on the mantel in the parlor next to the clock. As Christmas drew nearer, sounds of caroling grew merrier, the smell of

he was all alone in his cold, dark house, while every day the sounds of Christmas went on all around him.

The cuckoo flapped his wooden wings dutifully and roused himself to announce the hour. As his clock door opened, a blast of snowy wind hit the parlor windows and set the sash swinging. Ushered in on the snowflakes was a beautiful white dove. A real bird! The dove nodded and hopped toward the startled cuckoo and said, "The Christkind has sent me to tell you that she has heard your wish; and though she cannot promise for sure, she . . ." His words were lost in a gust of bitter wind as the curtains began whipping around the window frame, and in a flurry of white wings, the dove was swept back into the blizzard as suddenly as he had come.

The cuckoo was very curious about the dove's message, but he waited patiently. Finally, Christmas Eve came. Father and the eldest boy brought the Christmas tree into the parlor late that afternoon. Mother and the girls trimmed it with white wax candles, red velvet roses, and silver glass birds. Father read the story of the Christ Child and the last candle of the advent wreath was lit. The wreath was then placed in the window to guide the Christkind on her long, dark journey that night. And then all became silent. Not a whisper of wind was heard . . . not a crackle from the fireplace. Even the mice seemed to be fast asleep. Ten o'clock came and the bird cuckooed the hour. Eleven o'clock passed. Then the magic hour arrived.

The cuckoo heard the church bells pealing with joy. He, too, should announce the glad tidings. He opened his door a crack and saw that the room was flooded with a white light. He saw an angel with golden wings and on her shoulder was the white dove. She waved her wand over the Christmas tree and all the candles began to glow. She waved her wand again and brightly wrapped gifts appeared under the tree.

gingerbread sweeter, the warmth of the hearth cheerier, and the hearts of the children lighter. But the cuckoo grew sadder and sadder. Mother was so busy she forgot to wind the clock as often as needed, and for hours on end the cuckoo would be trapped inside his house not knowing whether it was day or night.

Only the weather was as bleak and desolate as the cuckoo. One night—the coldest night of the year—a blizzard blew through the village. Mother and father and all the children snuggled deep within their feather beds and were fast asleep. The cuckoo nestled shivering inside his clock, trying to remember the warm summer at the clockmaker's cottage. He thought of how the wooden birds had chattered among themselves and called to the real birds perched at the open windows. Why hadn't the clockmaker carved a little wooden quail friend for his clock so he would not be so lonely? Certainly the stiff wooden soldiers who guarded his balcony were luckier than he. Boring though they were, they at least had each other's company. But

The Christkind turned and smiled kindly toward the clock. The cuckoo stepped out bravely. "Cuckoo!" he called. "Cuckoo!" again.

"Cuc . . ." He caught his breath, his beak open in astonishment. Something was tugging on his pendulum! He looked down. A tiny mouse

with a large grin waved up at him.

"Merry Christmas, Brother Cuckoo!" he shouted. Other small mice then began to scramble up the chains of the clock, laughing and singing and calling out "Merry Christmas" to him. They crawled on his roof and swung from the hands of his clock. They hoisted up ribbons and garlands and sprigs of holly, and soon there was not a wooden leaf or bird left undecorated. Two mice tied a fat red satin ribbon around the carved reindeer's neck and another mouse plunked a red candied cherry on the reindeer's nose. "Come down! Come down!" called the mice on the floor to the cuckoo.

The Christkind laughed and waved her wand. The room came alive. The silver birds on the tree began to fly around the room. The gingerbread men on the sideboard began a Bavarian dance, and even the stiff soldiers on the clock's balcony broke into a rousing chorus of an old marching song. The cuckoo flew down to join his new mouse friends. How wonderful the night was, as well as the day to follow.

The children were up early and by the time the mother and father came downstairs most of the presents had been torn open and the parlor filled with colored paper. Father looked at the disarray and asked, "What time is it?" The youngest daughter looked up at the clock. "Look, Papa!" she cried. "The Christkind has trimmed the cuckoo clock."

That night—and every night after—as soon as everyone was asleep, the mice came to visit the cuckoo. They became the best of friends, and passed long winter nights spinning mouse lore.

The cuckoo, for his part, recounted the fairy tales he had heard at the clockmaker's cottage. His little wooden heart beat with such gladness and love that he sang out the hours of the days as if every day were Christmas, for of all the gifts we can receive, on Christmas or any day of the year, isn't friendship the best gift of all?

The Night Before Christmas

'Twas the night before Christmas, when all through the house
Not a creature was stirring, not even a mouse;
The stockings were hung by the chimney with care,
In hopes that St. Nicholas soon would be there;
The children were nestled all snug in their beds,
While visions of sugarplums danced in their heads;

And Mama in her 'kerchief, and I in my cap,
Had just settled our brains for a long winter's nap;
When out on the lawn there arose such a clatter,
I sprang from the bed to see what was the matter.
Away to the window I flew like a flash,
Tore open the shutters and threw up the sash.

The moon, on the breast of the new-fallen snow,
Gave the lustre of midday to objects below,
When what to my wondering eyes should appear,
But a miniature sleigh, and eight tiny reindeer,
With a little old driver, so lively and quick,
I knew in a moment it must be St. Nick.

More rapid than eagles his coursers they came,
And he whistled and shouted, and called them by name;
'Now, Dasher! Now, Dancer! Now, Prancer and Vixen!
On, Comet! On, Cupid! On, Donner and Blitzen!
To the top of the porch! To the top of the wall!
Now, dash away! Dash away! Dash away all!'

As dry leaves that before the wild hurricane fly,
When they meet with an obstacle, mount to the sky;
So up to the housetop the coursers they flew,
With the sleigh full of toys, and St. Nicholas, too.

And then, in a twinkling, I heard on the roof
The prancing and pawing of each little hoof—
As I drew in my head, and was turning around,
Down the chimney St. Nicholas came with a bound.

He was dressed all in fur, from his head to his foot,
And his clothes were all tarnished with ashes and soot;
A bundle of toys he had flung on his back,
And he looked like a pedlar just opening his pack.
His eyes—how they twinkled! His dimples, how merry!
His cheeks were like roses, his nose like a cherry!